Welcome to ALADDIN QUIX!

If you are looking for fast, fun-to-read stories with colorful characters, lots of kid-friendly humor, easy-to-follow action, entertaining story lines, and lively illustrations, then **ALADDIN QUIX** is for you!

But wait, there's more!

If you're also looking for stories with tables of contents; word lists; about-the-book questions; 64, 80, or 96 pages; short chapters; short paragraphs; and large fonts, then **ALADDIN QUIX** is *definitely* for you!

ALADDIN QUIX: The next step between ready to reads and longer, more challenging chapter books, for readers five to eight years old.

Read more ALADDIN QUIX books!

Our Principal Is a Frog!
by Stephanie Calmenson

A Miss Mallard Mystery: Dig to Disaster
by Robert Quackenbush

A Miss Mallard Mystery: Texas Trail to Calamity
by Robert Quackenbush

ROYAL SWEETS

A Royal Rescue

By Helen Perelman

Illustrated by Olivia Chin Mueller

ALADDIN QUIX

New York   London   Toronto   Sydney   New Delhi

To the Berkman family for being royally helpful readers
—H. P.

ALADDIN QUIX
Simon & Schuster Children's Publishing Division
1230 Avenue of the Americas, New York, New York 10020
First Aladdin QUIX paperback edition May 2018
Text copyright © 2018 by Helen Perelman
Illustrations copyright © 2018 by Olivia Chin Mueller
Also available in an Aladdin QUIX hardcover edition.
All rights reserved, including the right of reproduction in whole or in part in any form.
ALADDIN and the related marks and colophon
are trademarks of Simon & Schuster, Inc.
For information about special discounts for bulk
purchases, please contact Simon & Schuster Special Sales
at 1-866-506-1949 or business@simonandschuster.com.
The Simon & Schuster Speakers Bureau can bring authors to your live event. For
more information or to book an event contact the Simon & Schuster Speakers Bureau
at 1-866-248-3049 or visit our website at www.simonspeakers.com.
Cover designed by Jessica Handelman
Interior designed by Heather Palisi and Jessica Handelman
The illustrations for this book were rendered digitally.
The text of this book was set in Archer Medium.
Manufactured in the United States of America 1018 OFF
2 4 6 8 10 9 7 5 3
This book has been cataloged with the Library of Congress.
ISBN 978-1-4814-9478-6 (hc)
ISBN 978-1-4814-9477-9 (pbk)
ISBN 978-1-4814-9479-3 (eBook)

Cast of Characters

Princess Mini: Royal fairy princess of Candy Kingdom

Princess Lolli and Prince Scoop: Princess Mini's parents and ruling fairies of Candy Kingdom

Princess Taffy: Princess Mini's best friend

Lady Dot and Duke of Syrup: Princess Taffy's parents

Prince Frosting and Princess Cupcake: Princess Mini's twin cousins from Cake Kingdom

Princess Sprinkle: Princess Mini's aunt and ruler of Cake Kingdom

Princess Flour: Princess Mini's older cousin

Lady Cherry: Teacher at Royal Fairy Academy

Beanie: Royal chef

Butterscotch: Princess Mini's royal unicorn

Gobo: Troll living in Sugar Valley

Sir Nougat: Teacher at Royal Fairy Academy

Princess Swirlie: Princess Cupcake's best friend

Lord Licorice: Music teacher at Royal Fairy Academy

Chipper: Princess Taffy's royal unicorn

Sugarpop: Prince Frosting's royal unicorn

Contents

1

Super Stuck

"Happy first day of school, **Princess Mini!**" my mother said. She flew into my room with a big smile on her face.

My dad was behind her. "How's my first-year student?" he asked.

"Good," I said. Today I was extra excited. It was my first day at Royal Fairy Academy.

I was so nervous. My wings had not stopped **fluttering** fast all morning!

"First days are hard," my mom said. "Even for a fairy princess."

My parents were **Princess Lolli** and **Prince Scoop**, the ruling royal fairies in Candy Kingdom in Sugar Valley.

Being a fairy princess was really fun. And so was making all

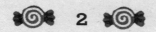

kinds of candy! I was a Chocolate Fairy. I could make chocolate chips with a simple touch, but I've made some messy mistakes.

My mom placed my **tiara** on my head.

"Don't worry. Taffy, Frosting, and Cupcake will be with you."

Princess Taffy was my best friend. We've been best friends since we were babies.

She was from nearby Sugar Kingdom. Her parents, **Lady Dot** and **Duke of Syrup**, were good friends with my parents.

Prince Frosting and **Princess Cupcake** were my cousins from Cake Kingdom. Their mom was my aunt, **Princess Sprinkle**, who ruled Cake Kingdom. Prince

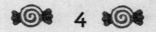

Frosting and Princess Cupcake were twins and as different as vanilla and chocolate.

Princess Cupcake was **prim**, proper, and a real pain. Prince Frosting was full of tricks and giving last licks. Being in class with them was *not* so sweet. Even though they were my cousins, we didn't always get along.

Their older sister, **Princess Flour**, had told us how strict and sometimes sour **Lady Cherry** was with first-years at Royal Fairy Academy.

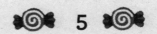

This made my wings twitch more.

My parents flew me down to the castle gate. **Beanie**, the royal chef, handed me my lunch in a small bucket.

"I put some special sweet treats for you in your lunch, Princess Mini," Beanie said.

Beanie was the best. She made the most **scrumptious** treats.

"Thank you," I replied. I climbed up on **Butterscotch**. The royal unicorn's mane was the color of pink cotton candy.

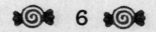

"See you later, sweetie," my mom called.

My dad waved and blew a royal kiss.

I held on tight to Butterscotch's mane. She flapped her large wings, and we were off.

Butterscotch flew over Chocolate River. Royal Fairy Academy was at the top of Chocolate Falls.

I could see the tall towers of the sugar-stone building and the colorful flags in the courtyard.

My heart and my wings started

to beat faster. These were my last
few moments of freedom!

I patted Butterscotch's mane to
slow her down.

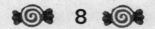

Just then I heard a cry.

Butterscotch's ears shot up straight. She must have heard the sound too.

"Is someone hurt?" I called. I patted her again. I landed Butterscotch in a clearing. The rushing waterfall was loud, but I could still hear a small voice calling out.

"Help! Help!"

"I would like to help you," I said, looking around. "But I can't see you." I flew to the ground. I

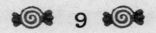

peered under the chocolate chew bushes and up at the chocolate oak tree.

There was a **crunch** behind me. I turned.

There on the ground, hiding behind a large chocolate oak leaf, was a tiny **troll**.

I had only ever seen trolls in books. I had never seen one face-to-face.

This troll was very small. He was wearing brown cut off shorts

and a white shirt with chocolate
stains on his belly. His white hair
was sticking up. And he was super
stuck in a caramel thornbush!

I knew I had to get to school. But I also knew I could not leave.

I bowed. "I am Princess Mini," I said. "I would like to help you."

2

Tricky Spot

The troll stared at me. Maybe he had never seen a Candy Fairy princess before. He looked me up and down.

"I'm stuck in a caramel thornbush," he said finally.

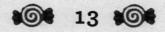

"I see," I said. "I once had a caramel thorn in my hand. My dad pulled it out."

"Oh," the little troll gasped. "Your—your—your dad, the fairy prince?" he stuttered.

"Do you know him?" I asked.

"Not exactly," he said, and shrugged. "I have heard stories from other trolls. He is very kind."

I moved a little closer. "What is your name?" I asked.

The troll's voice was quiet. I could barely hear him.

"My name is **Gobo**," he said. "But you shouldn't talk to me. We will both get into trouble."

I laughed. "Trouble? How can I get into trouble for helping you?" I said, and stood straighter. "I know I am just a first-year at Royal Fairy Academy, but fairy princesses are supposed to help others."

Gobo hung his head. "I'm not a fairy. I'm a troll," he said. "You should not be speaking to me."

"Who said that?" I asked boldly.

"I am not supposed to be here," he said. He looked up at me.

I looked closely at this little troll. He didn't seem to be making any trouble. "Were you stealing candy?" I asked.

"No," Gobo said. "I just wanted to explore."

"I love exploring too," I told him. "I can help. All I need is a drop of icing to pull you out of those caramel thorns," I said.

Luckily, Beanie had packed a cupcake in my lunch bucket.

"Here, take my hand," I said. "The icing will make it easier to pull you out."

Gobo reached forward. I pulled as hard as I could.

He came flying out of the bush.

POP!

"You did it!" Gobo said. "Thank you."

"Sure as sugar!" I told him happily.

Gobo smiled. His teeth were a little crooked.

"Now, stay away from the caramel thornbush," I said.

"I will," Gobo answered. He rubbed his sore bottom.

"Maybe we can explore together another time," I said.

"That would be fun," he agreed, and he looked up.

A bell had rung in the **distance**.

"Are you going to Royal Fairy Academy today?" he asked.

I nodded. "Yes, today is my first day," I said.

"You'd better hurry," he said, pointing to the school. "Those bells ring loudly when school starts."

"Oh, sour sticks!" I cried. "I can't be late on my first day!" I flew onto Butterscotch's back.

"Gobo, I will come back later, after school," I told him.

I waved to the little troll as Butterscotch flapped her large wings up into the sky.

I arrived at the school just as the last bell rang. I slid into line next to Taffy. I had made it!

3

Candy Lessons

"Good morning, students," said Lady Cherry. She opened the school doors.

"Welcome, Princess Mini," she said when she saw me. "I'm glad you got here on time."

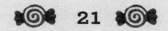

Lady Cherry knew my parents well. I had never met her, but she knew me.

I straightened my tiara and smiled. "Good morning, Lady Cherry," I said sweetly.

"Why were you late?" Taffy whispered to me.

"Wait till you hear," I said.

"Hear what?" It was my cousin Prince Frosting. He was standing right behind me. "I want to know why you were late."

I shot him a sour look.

"Hello, Prince Frosting," I said, trying to be sweet even though he made me feel bitter.

Princess Cupcake turned around. She flipped her long blond hair.

"No talking in line!" my cousin snapped at me.

Taffy took my hand. "Come on, Mini," she said. "Let's go!"

We entered a bright-lemon room with a huge window. I could see Chocolate Falls and the clearing where I had met Gobo.

Lady Cherry's long red dress and white apron swished as she flew around the room. "Come, students," she said. "Please sit down on the carpet for **attendance**."

All the fairies took a seat on the purple fruit-leather carpet.

"I'd like to welcome you all to our classroom," Lady Cherry said. She held a large scroll and a lollipop pen as she checked off our names. "I am very glad you are here. Now please find your

name on a desk and have a seat."

I was so happy my desk was next to Taffy's. I leaned over to her. "I have to tell you what happened on my way to school!"

"You'll have to wait to tell Taffy all about your morning adventure," Lady Cherry said **sternly**.

She tilted her dark head with its perfectly swirled bun. "Right now it's time for your candy lesson with **Sir Nougat**."

"Yes, Lady Cherry," I said. I kept my eyes lowered. I didn't want to get into trouble on my first day.

"Let's show our best royal behavior for Sir Nougat," Lady Cherry said. "His lesson is about sugar and spice."

Prince Frosting shot out of his seat. **"I'm ready for some super spice,"** he declared.

"Perhaps a little more sugar," Lady Cherry said, sighing.

At nine on the dot Sir Nougat appeared in the doorway.

He flew over to my desk. He had a wide smile and very blue eyes. "It's a treat to have you here, Mini," he said.

"Thank you," I said. I didn't love the idea that all the teachers knew who I was already. But having parents who were the ruling fairies of Candy Kingdom, I knew to expect that.

"Is it time to spice things up?" Frosting asked.

"Yes," Sir Nougat said. He placed a large bowl of sugar on the front desk.

"This year you will learn about different types of candy. For our first lesson we will try sugar and spice." He took out a bag full of spice ingredients for us to use. "Try adding cinnamon or a dash of mint. Have fun!"

All the royals in the class were busy making sugar-and-spice candy. I wasn't sure what to do. I looked out the window.

I wondered what Gobo was

doing. Was he still exploring? Had he kept away from the thorny caramel bushes?

"Princess Mini, are you listening?" Sir Nougat asked. He was standing in front of my desk.

"I'm . . . I'm . . . having a little trouble," I said. I felt my face grow red.

"Sugar and spice is one of the main **themes** of making candy this year," he said. "I suggest you pay attention."

Frosting leaned over to my

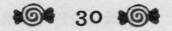

desk. "Mini, getting in trouble already?"

"Mind your own business," Taffy snapped.

"Thanks, Taffy," I said. I swirled some sugar and cinnamon in my sugar bowl. Tiny cinnamon chocolate chips appeared. "Sugar and spice," I declared proudly.

"**Wow!**" Taffy said. "Nice job." She reached over for a taste of my mini–cinnamon chocolate chips.

It might have been my first day, but I could make sugar-and-spice candy.

"**Sweet!**" Frosting said. But the way he said it didn't sound so sweet.

Taffy took a bite of her spicy taffy. She made a face. "**Oh, too much spice!**" she said.

She spit out her candy. "School is hard." She sighed and pulled back her dark wavy hair off her face.

"School is harder than I thought," I agreed.

"Let's not get our wings so low," Taffy whispered. "Recess is next! And we'll be great at that!"

4

Sticky and Icky

When the bell rang to end Sir Nougat's lesson, the fairies all raced out to the courtyard.

Princess Cupcake came over with **Princess Swirlie**, her best friend from Ice Cream Isles.

They were a perfect blend of icy, sweet sugar.

"Hello," I said. I was trying to use my best royal manners. But when I saw their sour faces, it was hard to be sweet.

"My sister told me Sir Nougat

doesn't like the same old candy every time," Cupcake told me. "Just a friendly warning: you can't just make chocolate chips all the time."

"Super sugar dress," Swirlie said, rolling her eyes. She followed Cupcake to the other side of the yard.

Taffy put her hand on my shoulder. "Don't worry about them," she said. "They are double trouble."

"Sticky and icky," I said.

The colorful playground was

full of fairies playing on rainbow-leather slides, caramel swings, and long licorice ropes.

Taffy and I sat under the large gummy tree on the side of the school courtyard.

"So tell me what happened this morning," Taffy said.

As I told Taffy the story about Gobo, I was careful to watch for other fairies. I didn't want anyone else to hear about him.

"This is so exciting," Taffy said. "I've never met a troll!"

"I know," I said. "Will you come with me after school to check on him?"

"Sure as sugar!" Taffy said.

Just then I saw Prince Frosting fly by.

"What is happening after school?" he asked.

I wasn't sure how much he had heard.

The bells in the tall sugar tower rang, and we all headed back into class.

"Oh, Mini." Taffy sighed. "We will have to be very careful. We don't want the whole class knowing about this."

"You're right," I agreed. "We'll have to make sure that no one follows us after school."

We flew back to the classroom. I wondered what Prince Frosting had heard. And what he would do if he learned about Gobo.

5

Keeping Secrets

After recess my wings finally slowed down.

I was starting to feel more comfortable at school. I was still unsure about making different types of candy, but I was doing

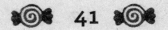

okay. Plus, Taffy and I had a plan to see Gobo, and so far our secret was safe.

Then Frosting came up to me in **Lord Licorice**'s music class.

"What are you up to, Mini?" Frosting asked.

"Nothing," I said.

I didn't love singing, but I was happy when the music finally started. I wouldn't have to answer any more questions from nosy Frosting.

"Sing it out," Lord Licorice said. He sat at a sugarcoated piano. He played with one hand and conducted with the other.

After music the class returned to Lady Cherry's lemon-colored room. The lesson was how to make chocolate balls.

I was glad this candy was pure chocolate!

"Nice work, Mini," Lady Cherry said. She smiled at my row of chocolate balls.

"One for your cousin?" Frosting asked. He leaned over my desk with a goofy grin.

I handed Frosting one of the chocolates. "Here," I said. If he was chewing, then he wouldn't be asking me questions!

Frosting had a plateful of messy globs of chocolate—unlike Princess Cupcake, who was still working on rolling her candy into perfect balls.

"You don't get a prize for finishing first," Cupcake said. She made a sour face at Frosting and me.

"No, but we do get to eat it first!" Frosting said, slurping up one of his chocolates.

"Any big plans after school?" Cupcake asked. She always loved to know everyone's business.

"Taffy is coming over to the castle," I said.

Ding-dong, ding-dong!

The large bells in the tower rang. The first day of school was over!

All the fairies lined up and flew out to the courtyard.

The royal unicorns were all waiting patiently for their royal passengers.

"I'm going to find out what

you are up to," Frosting said.

"We're not up to anything," I replied.

"Humph!" he said. "We'll see about that!"

Frosting gave me a long hard stare. "You have another plan," he said. "I want to know what it is."

Princess Cupcake flew over. "Oh, this is so boring," she said. "Come on, Frost. Let's go to Sour Forest with the others. At least they know how to have fun."

She nodded to the group of fairies waiting for them. "Mini and Taffy are so bland."

"I'm not sure about that," Frosting said.

He turned back to me. "I'm watching you, Mini," he added. "I know there is something **sugar-tastic** that you don't want me to know."

After they left, Taffy said, "Well, we know he doesn't know

about Gobo." She climbed up onto her unicorn, **Chipper**. "He would have said something."

"Now I hope we can keep Gobo from him," I said.

6

Forever Friends

Butterscotch and Chipper flew to the clearing near Chocolate Falls. I didn't see any sign of Gobo.

"Gobo," I called. "Are you there? It's me, Princess Mini."

There was no answer.

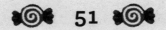

"Maybe he left?" Taffy asked.

"Maybe he is scared," I said.

Then I had a yummy idea!

I took out the chocolate balls that I had made at school. I lined them up on the ground.

"A troll can't **resist** candy," I said. "Come and let's wait behind the chocolate oak," I told Taffy.

Taffy and I hid behind the old, thick tree. We waited and waited.

Finally I saw him! He was slowly sneaking out from under a bush. He took the chocolates!

"Hello, Gobo," I said, flying out
to see him, but I felt a pull on my
right wing. I couldn't move.

"Oh," I cried. I tried to flutter my wings. I was stuck!

"Mini, you're caught on a caramel leaf," Taffy said. "Hold on."

Before Taffy could move, Gobo

took a leap and landed on a low tree branch next to me. He squeezed icing on my wings. I wiggled free.

I flew up into the sky and shook my wings. "Thank you, Gobo," I said. "That icing saved me!"

"Now I know to keep some icing handy around the Caramel Woods," Gobo said.

"You both saved each other from sticky situations," Taffy said. "This is the start of a very sweet friendship."

Gobo started to shake. "Who...

who . . . who is that?" he asked. He pointed to Taffy, who had come out from behind the tree.

"This is Princess Taffy from Sugar Kingdom. Her mom is Lady Dot and her father is Duke of Syrup," I said.

Taffy bowed.

"She is my best friend," I said. "You can trust her."

"Hello, Gobo," Taffy said. "We came to check on you and see if you were okay."

"All good," he said, rubbing

his bottom. "Did you make it to school on time?" Gobo asked.

I laughed. "Just barely," I told him. "I have to work on being on time and listening to directions. I am not used to being in school."

"Me either," Gobo said.

I stepped closer to Gobo. "Do *you* go to school too?" I asked.

Gobo shook his head. "There is no troll school," he said. "I wish there was so I could learn how to make candy."

"Sweet cocoa!" I yelled.

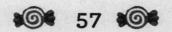

"Taffy and I can teach you!"

"Sure as sugar," Taffy said. "Would you like that, Gobo?"

But Gobo didn't answer.

In a flash he had disappeared under a caramel bush.

"I knew you two were up to something!" Frosting called. He flew above us on his unicorn, **Sugarpop**.

Princess Cupcake and Princess Swirlie were sitting behind him on the unicorn.

I should have known Prince

 58

Frosting would not have come alone.

"What's the big secret?" Princess Cupcake asked.

"Who were you talking to?" Prince Frosting said.

I was glad that Gobo was so fast.

"Taffy and I just wanted to **practice** sugar-and-spice recipes," I said.

Princess Cupcake flipped her hair. "I don't believe that," she said. "But it doesn't look like anyone else is here." She looked over at Frosting. "You made us leave Sour Forest for *this*?"

"This is boring," Princess Swirlie said with a sigh.

"I guess we are boring," I said, winking at Taffy.

Frosting patted Sugarpop's mane. "I still think you two are hiding something."

"See you tomorrow at school," I said, waving as Sugarpop flew off. **"Pssssssst!"** I whispered. "They're gone, Gobo. It's okay to come out now."

"That was too close," Gobo said. He crawled out of hiding. "I have seen those royals before. I think they hoped to find me stealing candy."

He sat down on a caramel rock.

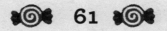

"Even when I wasn't stealing."

"We can protect you," I said bravely.

"You can?" Gobo said. He looked at Taffy and then me. "Why would you want to help me?"

I put my hands on my hips.

"Because you live in my king-dom," I said. "And I am your fairy princess . . . in training."

Gobo smiled a toothy grin. "I am glad to hear that."

"I rescued you once," I said. "And I would do it again."

"I think we're going to be supersweet friends," Taffy told Gobo.

"Friends through **sticky and sweet**," I said.

"And thorny spots," Gobo said.

"Friends till the end," Taffy said.

I put out my pinkie. "Let's hook pinkies and make a promise."

Gobo held up his chubby pinkie. Then Taffy put out her pinkie. We linked our fingers as we stood in a circle.

"To a sweet secret friendship!" I exclaimed.

My wings started to flutter, and this time it was because I was so happy—not nervous. The day started with me feeling scared, but it ended with a new friend and promises of fun adventures.

"To many adventures together!" I said to Taffy and Gobo.

Word List

attendance (a·TEN·dents): A record of the number of people (or fairies) present

distance (DIS·tents): Something far away from a point or place

fluttering (FLUT·tur·ing): Moving wings fast

practice (PRAK·tis): To do something again and again to be better at it

prim (PRIM): Very formal and proper

resist (ree·ZIST): To stop yourself from doing something you want to do

scrumptious (SKRUMP·shus): Very tasty or delicious

sternly (STURN·lee): Very seriously

themes (THEEMZ): Main ideas

tiara (tee·AR·a): A small crown often worn by princesses or queens

troll (TROL): A dwarf who lives in caves in hills

Questions

1. What type of fairy is Princess Mini?

2. How is Princess Mini's school the same as or different from your school?

3. Where does Princess Mini find Gobo the troll?

4. How does Princess Mini help Gobo out of a sticky spot?

5. What kind of adventures do you think Gobo and Princess Mini will have together?